lily & limbo

Where Flowers Go

Written by
Leslie Vilhelmsen

Illustrated by
Laura Goodman

Balboa Press books may be ordered through booksellers or by contacting:

Balboa Press
A Division of Hay House
1663 Liberty Drive
Bloomington, IN 47403
www.balboapress.com
1 (877) 407-4847

Interior Image Credit: Laura Goodman

ISBN: 978-1-9822-4502-3 (sc)
ISBN: 978-1-9822-4503-0 (e)

Library of Congress Control Number: 2020904981

Print information available on the last page.

Balboa Press rev. date: 05/01/2020

BALBOA.PRESS
A DIVISION OF HAY HOUSE

To Mom
Leslie Vilhelmsen

To my two beautiful children,
Eligh and Magdalene
Laura Goodman

Credits:
Written by: Leslie Vilhelmsen
Illustrated by: Laura Goodman

Lily and Limbo

Mother had a gentle,
heartfelt talk with Julia.

A tearful Julia ran outdoors.

Seeking comfort from
her favorite tree,
she hugged Limbo.

Julia shared that her
grandmother has died.

Limbo comforted Julia
with a story about
his friend Lily.

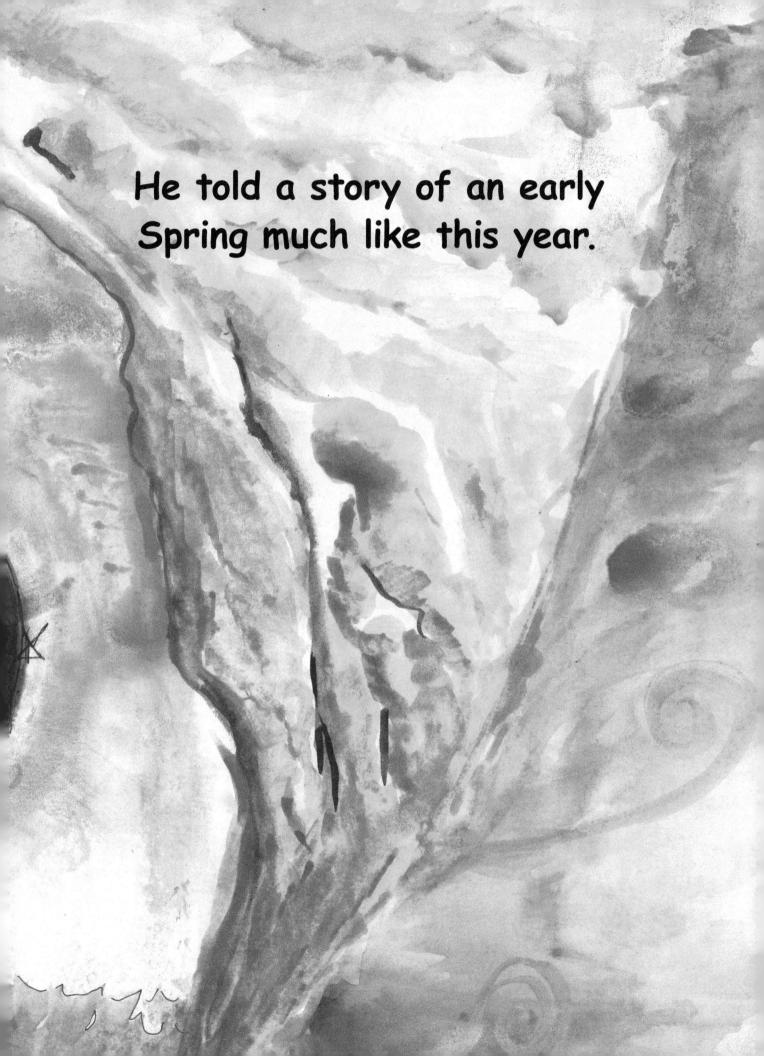

He told a story of an early
Spring much like this year.

Lily was so
joyful, she
attracted
many
creatures.

Nutz and Chatter, the squirrels,
provided entertainment.

A pair of deer, Aspen and
Kaiya, gently greeted Lily.

Grande, the robin, built a nest
in Limbo's sturdy branches.

All enjoyed Grande's
daily songs.

In Spring, Lily saved
a falling baby bird.

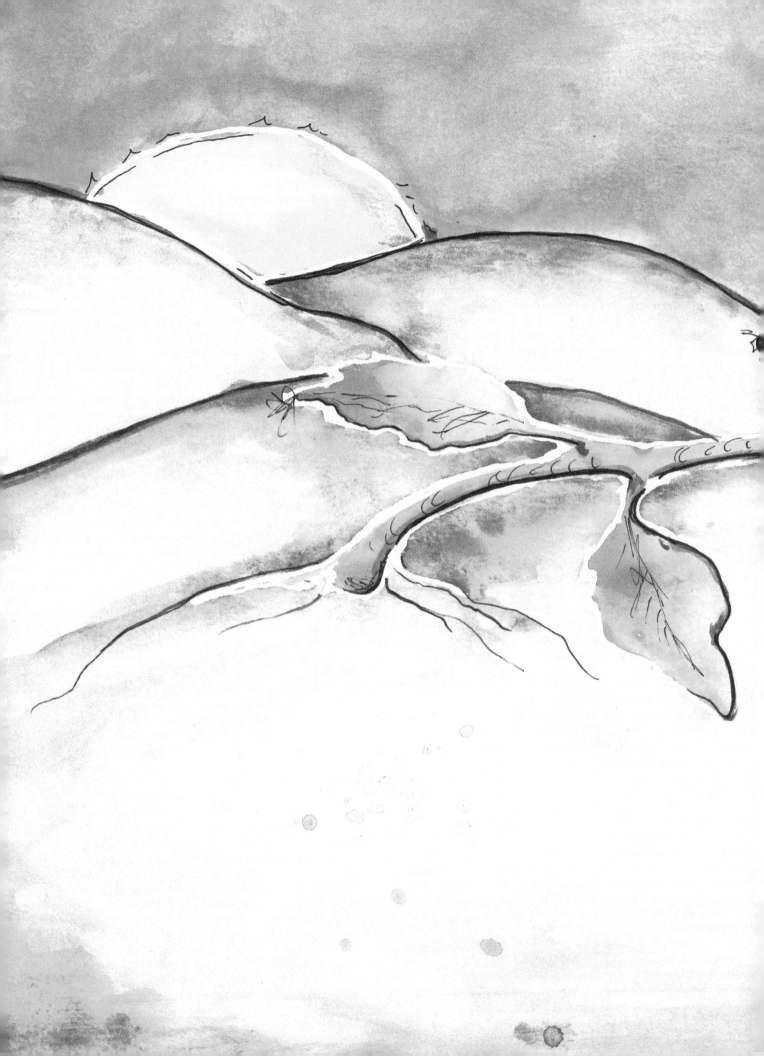

Lily dreamed she could
fly like the birds.

When Bumble and
Buzz tickled her,
Lily giggled.

Olga told stories under the twinkling summer stars.

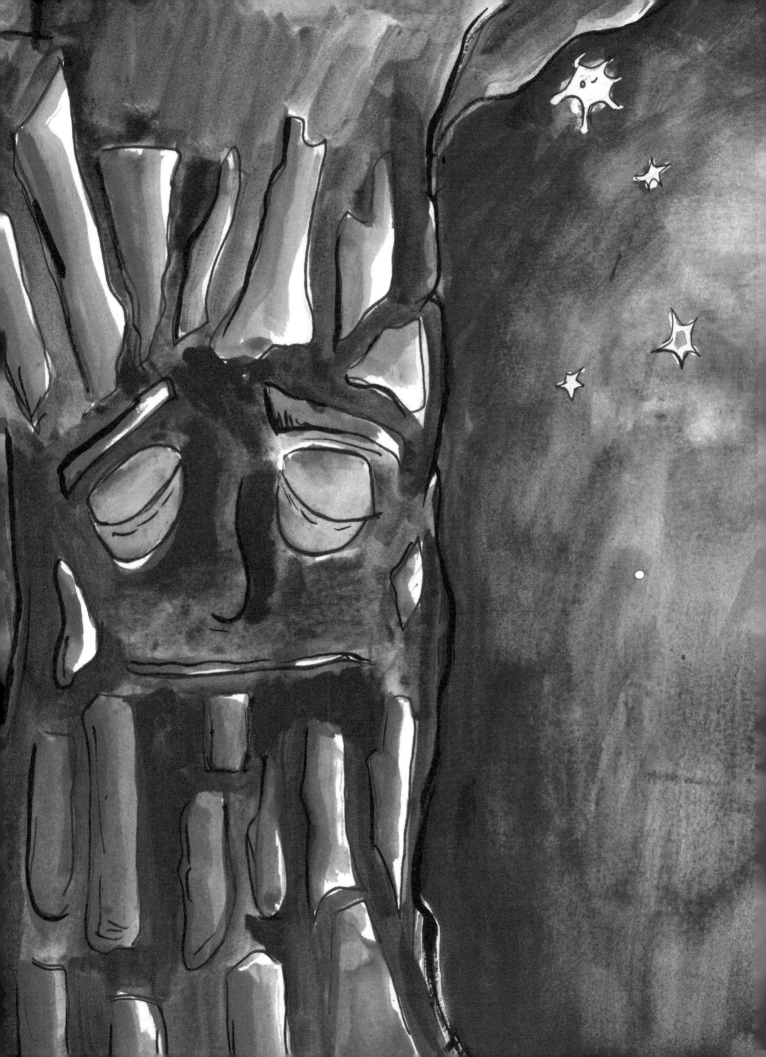

These were very special times.

Each morning
the moon melted
away when the
sun appeared.

Seasons change
as seasons do.

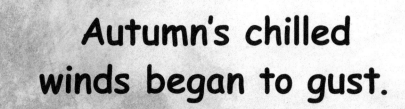

Autumn's chilled
winds began to gust.

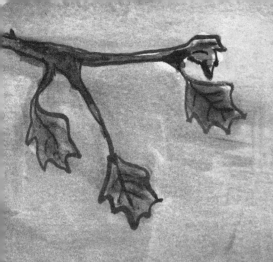

Lily's smallest
friends hugged her
like a warm blanket

Limbo used his
nearly bare branches
to protect Lily
from the frost.

All their friends came to say goodbye to Lily.

They shared the special place
Lily had in their lives.

Olga said, "While the sky may be dark now, daylight will follow."

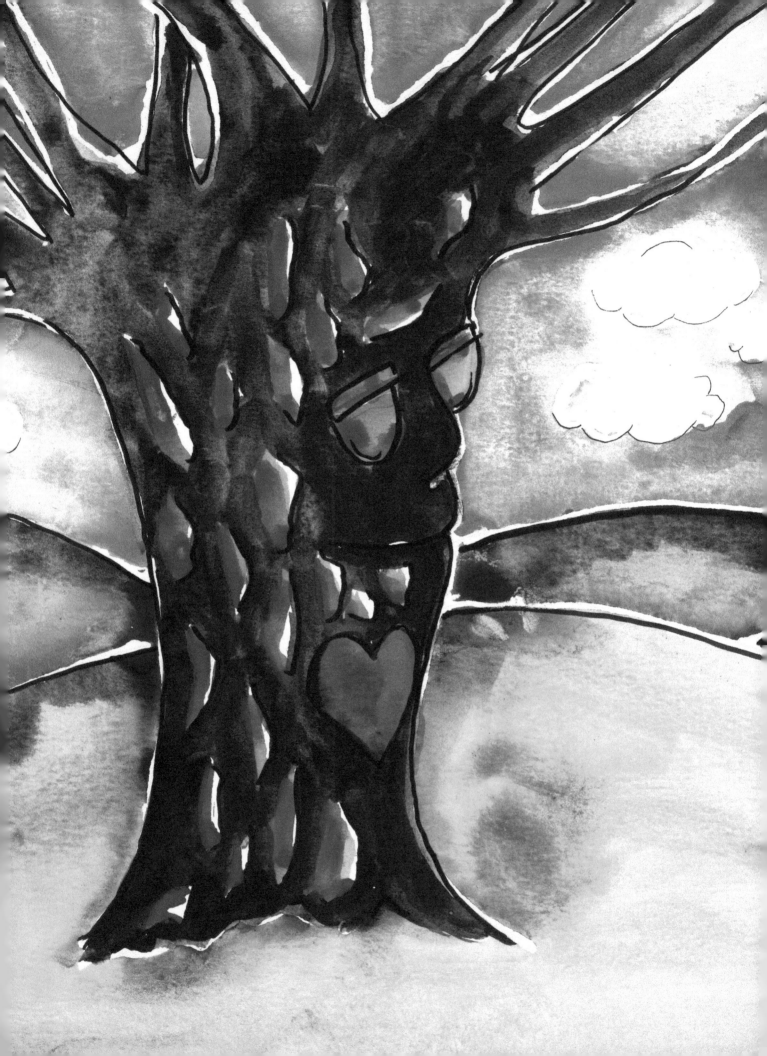

Limbo added, "Lily, I will always remember you."

Limbo said to Julia, "Lily will always be a part of my heart."

We are all flowers in the garden of life. All flowers have a special purpose and unique gift to share.

Some flowers live many seasons,
but others are like shooting stars....
brilliant but gone too soon.

Once we have shared our special
gifts the journey is complete,
and we can say goodbye.

About The Author

Leslie Vilhelmsen was once an accomplished competitive ice skater. She is an amazing chocolatier as well a painter using an oil-based medium. Leslie currently resides in Charlotte, NC.

Laura Goodman is inspired by nature and works predominantly in acrylic paints and water; creating imagery reflecting a whimsical and mysterious style. Laura resides in Rock Hill, SC.

CPSIA information can be obtained
at www.ICGtesting.com
Printed in the USA
LVHW071130120520
655425LV00027B/2874

9 781982 245023